Look for more

titles:

TWO of a kind™
Diaries
Island Girls

by Nancy Butcher
from the series created by
Robert Griffard & Howard Adler

HarperEntertainment
An Imprint of HarperCollinsPublishers
A PARACHUTE PRESS BOOK

A PARACHUTE PRESS BOOK

Parachute Publishing, L.L.C.
156 Fifth Avenue
New York, NY 10010

Published by
▰HarperEntertainment

An Imprint of HarperCollins*Publishers*
10 East 53rd Street, New York, NY 10022-5299

TWO OF A KIND books created and produced by Parachute Press, L.L.C., in cooperation with Dualstar Publications, a division of Dualstar Entertainment Group, L.L.C., published by HarperEntertainment, an imprint of HarperCollins Publishers.

ISBN 0-06-106663-X

HarperCollins®,▰®, and HarperEntertainment™ are trademarks of HarperCollins Publishers Inc.

First printing: June 2002

Printed in the United States of America

Visit HarperEntertainment on the World Wide Web at
www.harpercollins.com

10 9 8 7 6 5 4 3 2 1

Chapter 1

Saturday

Dear Diary,

Aloha! That's how you say hello in Hawaiian. In a few minutes our plane will be landing at the airport in Hilo, Hawaii!

It's the first week of summer vacation and I'm on a school trip with some of my classmates from the White Oak Academy for Girls. White Oak is the boarding school in New Hampshire that I go to with my twin sister, Ashley. We're First Formers there (that means seventh-graders).

I can see long beaches and tall palm trees from the window of the plane. They're totally different from the green hills of New Hampshire. This trip is going to be awesome. Lots of my friends are here!

First there's Ashley's roommate, Phoebe Cahill, and my roommate and best bud, Campbell Smith (who's sitting next to me). There's also Julia Langstrom, Summer Sorenson, and Elise Van Hook.

Dana Woletsky is here, too. I kind of wish she *wasn't* here. She's a superpopular First Former and she's never been nice to Ashley or me. I hope I won't have to spend time with her on this trip!

1

Our group isn't just all girls. The Harrington School for Boys is down the road from White Oak, and they sent some of the guys to Hawaii, too! Grant Marino, Hans Jensen, Seth Samuels, and Devon Benjamin all came along. And I can't forget my cousin-dearest, Jeremy. He is so annoying! Diary, the only thing Ashley and I have in common with Jeremy is a last name.

"Hey, Mary-Kate," Jeremy said, walking up the aisle. "Hold this for a second, will you?"

I held out my hand. "Eeek!" I shrieked when he dropped something wiggly in my palm. Then I realized it was only a rubber spider.

Jeremy slapped his leg. "Ha! Gets 'em every time."

I threw the spider back at Jeremy. I hope he doesn't play practical jokes the whole time we're here. This trip is going to be a real challenge and practical jokes are the last thing we need!

We're going to Hawaii for four whole weeks. For the first half of our vacation we're participating in Wild Hawaii—a once-in-a-lifetime wilderness adventure, where we live off the land for twelve whole days. Imagine it, Diary—gathering food, building shelter, surviving on our own! Wow, it sounds even cooler now than when Ashley read me the description from the brochure!

For the second half of our vacation, we're off to an island resort, where our only responsibilities will be to relax and have fun!

Campbell elbowed me. "Did you know that certain kinds of flowers are edible?" she said. She was reading from a book called *The Outdoor Survival Guide*. Before we left for vacation, Campbell and I had gone to the school library to take out books on  camping in Hawaii. We wanted to make sure we were ready for anything!

I shook my head. "Nope. What else have you learned?"

Campbell jabbed her finger at another page. "That you can use the leaves of the aloe plant to treat minor burns and cuts."

I took a sip of the pineapple juice that the flight attendant had passed out. "Excellent! We'll totally be able to use all that information. Can I look through the books tonight?"

Campbell grinned. "Sure. After we finish reading these, we'll be experts at living in the wild."

It's a little scary to think that we'll be living the

way people did zillions of years ago, without electricity and Ben and Jerry's ice cream. (Just kidding about the ice cream, Diary.) But we'll have a Wild Hawaii guide to tell us what to do and to take us to cool places on the island. I can't wait!

"Ms. Clare, will there be someone to carry our suitcases at the airport?" Summer asked from across the aisle.

Ms. Clare is the assistant headmistress of White Oak. She's really nice. Mr. Turnbull, the assistant headmaster of Harrington, is here, too. When we  first met him, he was really mean and scary—but these days he's much more laid-back. Right now he's sitting a few rows in front of me trying to play the ukulele!

"Why do you ask?" Ms. Clare replied.

Summer flipped her long blond hair over her shoulders. "Because I brought, like, five or six suitcases."

Elise gasped. "Summer, Ms. Clare told us to pack *light*!"

Summer shrugged. "I thought I *was* packing light. Five suitcases isn't a lot of clothing."

Dana leaned across Summer and flashed me a

smile. "Speaking of clothing, that is such a cute sun-dress, Mary-Kate!"

"Um, thanks," I said slowly. *Dana giving me a compliment? Unbelievable*, I thought.

"It really hides those extra pounds," she added.

I took a deep breath and counted to ten. I didn't want to say anything that would get me in trouble.

"Mary-Kate! Smile and say something for the camera!"

I glanced up. Phoebe's head popped over the seat in front of me. She was holding a video camera. I could tell by the blinking red light near the lens that she was recording.

"Hey, everyone!" I said with a big wave. "Wish you were here!"

Phoebe has the coolest job on this vacation. She will be camping on the beach with us, but she's not part of the Wild Hawaii challenge. She's here to capture all the action on video. The footage will be shown at a special school assembly this fall. (I hope she doesn't catch me doing anything stupid!)

"Attention, passengers," the pilot announced over the loudspeaker. "Please fasten your seat belts."

Yay! We're almost ready to land. Hello, Hilo!

Two of a Kind Diaries

Dear Diary,

I am now officially a wilderness girl. And I have to tell you, it's not that bad!

Last night we stayed at the hotel. This morning Mr. Turnbull and Ms. Clare took us to the camp, which is about a mile away. They'll be with us only part of the time at Wild Hawaii. The rest of the time they'll stay at the hotel.

The camp is a big open area on the beach surrounded by palm trees. To our left is the ocean. To our right are a bunch of twisty trails lined with exotic plants and flowers.

Our guide's name is Maleko. That's how you say Mark in Hawaiian. (Maleko told me that my name in Hawaiian is Mai Ke!)

Maleko has long black hair that he wears back in a ponytail, and he has huge muscles. He must exercise ten hours a day or something. Maleko was dressed in denim cutoffs and a T-shirt that said NO FEAR. He wasn't wearing shoes.

"Wild Hawaii is not your typical vacation" were the first words out of Maleko's mouth. "Wild Hawaii is an experience that will challenge you physically, mentally, and emotionally."

"That doesn't sound like a vacation at all," Jeremy said.

"For the next twelve days you will be in survival mode," Maleko went on. "That means you will have limited supplies. Only a few articles of clothing and some camping gear."

"So much for Summer's five suitcases," Mary-Kate whispered to me.

Elise's brown eyes grew really wide. "Can we bring makeup?" she asked.

"No way." Maleko folded his arms across his chest.

"Not even *lip gloss*?" I asked. "Lip gloss is a big part of my life!"

"Not even lip gloss," Maleko replied.

"But this is a survival trip," Summer cut in. "How am I supposed to survive without makeup?"

Phoebe whipped her camera around, pointing it right at Summer. "Raw emotion! Good! Summer, please tell us how you feel about having to live without makeup for twelve days."

Summer's expression changed as soon as she saw the video camera. She plastered a big smile on her face. "I said, this is going to be a blast!" she exclaimed.

I giggled. Phoebe wrinkled her nose.

"Each of you will be given a job to do," Maleko continued, "like pitching tents and collecting food. Everyone must work as a team to survive. If you are not a team player or you don't complete your job for the day, you will be eliminated from the Wild Hawaii challenge and sent back to the hotel."

"That's a harsh rule," Seth commented.

"It didn't say that in the brochure," Dana added.

"When do we get to have fun?" I asked.

Maleko smiled. "The fun comes from knowing that you can survive in the wild. It's going to be tough at first, but at the end of the twelve days, you'll find out how strong you really are."

Maleko's words were starting to pump me up. I could tell everyone else was getting into the idea, too.

"You will see things on this island that you've never seen before," Maleko went on, "and you'll find a part of yourself that you never knew existed." He looked around at all of us. "Are you guys up for the challenge?"

"Yeah!" we all cried together.

"Good." Maleko nodded. "I haven't even told you the best part yet. Because teamwork is so important in Wild Hawaii, at the end of the twelve days the person who I think has demonstrated the

8

best teamwork will win a special prize."

Teamwork is my middle name, I thought. *And I am always up for a challenge—especially if it means winning something!* "What is the prize?" I asked.

"A one-hundred-dollar shopping spree in Hawaii," Maleko said.

Everyone started talking excitedly. "That prize is mine!" Hans announced.

"No way, dude," Grant told him. "*I'm* going to win."

I tapped Phoebe on the shoulder. She turned her video camera on me. "Yes?"

"You can get *this* on tape," I exclaimed. "The only person who is going to win that shopping spree is *me!*"

Chapter 2

Sunday

Dear Diary,

Ever since Maleko mentioned the hundred-dollar prize, everyone has been going out of their way to show that they are a team player. Hans offered to carry my backpack. Julia gave a few people some of her muffin from breakfast. Even Jeremy got in on the act and told jokes to keep up the group's spirits.

"Mary-Kate." Campbell joined me as I checked out the beach. "Don't you think we should tell the other kids what we learned from our survival guides?"

"Sure. That's what good team players would do," I agreed. I sat down on the sand. Nearby, a patch of orange orchids waved in the breeze.

I turned to Campbell as she sat next to me. "What would you buy if you won the hundred dollars?" I asked her.

Campbell grinned. "I would definitely hit the sports store at the hotel," she said.

"Me, too," I agreed. Campbell and I have a lot of things in common. That's one reason why we are such good friends.

"All right, people, gather around!" Maleko

waved to everyone and I saw the muscles ripple in his arm. Diary, that guy must *live* at the gym.

Campbell and I headed over to the group. We all sat down in a circle. Maleko held up his clipboard.

"I've divided you all into teams of two and three for each job," he explained.

Maleko slowly read off our names and jobs. Finally, he got to me. "Mary-Kate, you have fishing duty," he said. "Each day you have to catch the group's dinner. Campbell will be your partner."

Campbell and I high-fived. Fishing with my best friend. This was going to be great!

Of course, I'd been fishing only once in my life and that was when I was five. But how hard could it be?

Maleko said we had to make our own fishing poles. Normally, I would have panicked at the news. But Campbell and I read all about how to do it in one of our camping books!

"First, we should find some bamboo," Campbell suggested.

This took longer than we thought it would. But only because we stopped to help Julia carry some heavy pieces of wood. She was on firewood duty.

Once we found some long, skinny pieces of bamboo, we needed to find fishing line and hooks.

"Do you think Maleko brought us some?" I asked hopefully.

Campbell shook her head. "No way," she said. "But I bet someone has some dental floss. That might work as fishing line."

"What an excellent idea!" I said. "And we can borrow some paper clips from Phoebe to use as hooks. She always has some in her backpack."

"Mary-Kate, we are brilliant!" Campbell cheered.

When we were done making the fishing rods, we decided to use some sharp rocks to carve our initials into the bamboo. That way, we would be able to tell them apart. I felt really proud of myself, Diary! I was starting to feel at one with nature already.

On a less exciting note, we needed bait, so we had to pull slimy little worms out of the sand and put them in a small bucket. All I can really say about that is—yuck! We used some really big shells to dig with.

"So far so good," Campbell said when our bucket was full.

"Yeah, but now we actually have to *catch* the fish," I pointed out.

12

Campbell plunked down our bucket of bait and fishing poles into the wooden boat that Maleko had given us. "Don't worry, we can do it."

We put on our life jackets and climbed into the boat. Then we each took an oar. We paddled out to a small lagoon. I noticed Summer and Jeremy rustling through the bushes in the distance, picking berries. Summer didn't look too happy about it. I guess she wasn't as excited about the wilderness as I was.

The water was so clear all around us I could see schools of tiny yellow fish swimming near the surface.

"I am *not* eating those guys," I told Campbell, pointing at the fish. "They are way too cute!"

"Don't worry," Campbell said. "That's not what we're fishing for. They're too small."

We fished for about two hours. By the time we rowed back to shore we had caught ten big fish!

Campbell and I delivered the fish to Dana, Elise, and Seth. They were the cooking crew.

"Excellent!" Seth exclaimed. "We'll fry these babies up for dinner."

Thanks to some tips from our books, we helped the cooking crew get the fire started in no time at all. We even showed them how to clean the fish!

"You guys are really the best," Elise said. "I

definitely did not want to clean those fish myself."

We helped out a lot today, Diary. Maybe Campbell or I will even win the prize! But since we did everything together, I decided that if I won the prize, I would share it with Campbell.

"I was just thinking the same thing, MK!" she said when I told her.

Campbell and I are an awesome team.

Dear Diary,

Maleko put me, Hans, and Devon in charge of pitching tents for the whole group. (Maleko, aka Mr. Extreme, told us he never uses a tent. He would rather sleep in the open.)

"Have you guys ever been camping before?" I asked Hans and Devon.

"I've been camping with my family a few times," Devon replied. "But my parents usually put the tents together."

Hans shook his head. "I've never been camping before," he said. "How about you, Ashley?"

"I was in the Bluebird Scout Troop for five years and we went camping every year," I said. "We're in luck.

I'm a total *expert* at building tents."

"Excellent!" Hans said. "Then what should we do first?"

"That's easy," Devon said. "We put the poles together."

"Right," I agreed. "They make up the framework for the tent."

We each grabbed some poles and examined them. "What do these little red dots at the end of each pole mean?" Hans asked.

"I bet we're supposed to match them up to each other," Devon guessed.

I shook my head. "I've seen tents like this before," I explained. "I think this brand is just made with red dots at the end. We have to figure out ourselves which poles match up."

Devon shrugged. "Are you sure?" he asked doubtfully.

"Pretty sure," I replied.

"Then let's get started," Hans said. He reached for a few poles.

"Let me hold that up for you." I steadied a pole so Hans could attach it to another one.

"Thanks, Ashley," Hans said.

I smiled. Was this teamwork or what?

A few minutes later I snapped together the last

two poles. I stood between Devon and Hans as we all examined our work. "Looks good to me!" I said.

"I guess so," Devon said. He didn't look one hundred percent convinced. I knew he was still thinking about the dots. But he'd realize I was right once we were done.

"What's next?" Hans asked.

"Now we attach the tents to the poles," I said.

Devon picked up one of the tarps and threw it over the pole. But I knew from camping that you had to carefully attach certain pieces of the tent to each pole—not just throw it over.

"Devon, that's not how you do it," I said.

"Yes, it is," he insisted. "I definitely remember watching my parents do this part."

"It looks okay to me," Hans said, checking out the tarp.

"Guys, trust me," I replied. "I know what I'm talking about. Didn't I know how to put all the poles together?"

"But, Ashley—" Devon started.

"We have to focus on being a good team," I interrupted. "That means listening to one another."

Devon kicked a foot in the sand. "Fine. We'll do it your way."

"Thanks," I said. Once I showed the guys how to fasten the tents, it didn't take us long to finish them all.

"We're almost done!" I said excitedly. "All we have left is to put in the stakes."

"Even *I* know what to do with these," Hans said, picking up the bag of metal stakes. "We tie them to the tents and then pound them into the ground, right?"

"Well, sort of," I replied. "It's just the other way around. First you put the stakes into the ground and *then* you attach them to the tents."

"Are you sure, Ashley?" Devon asked. "That doesn't sound right to me. I think we should do it Hans's way."

"But I know I'm right about this," I replied. "That's how we used to do it at camp."

Devon scowled at me. Hans didn't look too happy either.

Maybe I should compromise, I thought. *That's what a good team player would do, right?* "Okay," I said. "Let's each do it our own way."

"Fine," Hans and Devon said together. We pounded the stakes in silence.

We finished just as the sun went down. I stood up and examined our work. A few of the tents were a little crooked—but they didn't look half bad!

"Congratulations, team," I said. "We did a great job."

Jeremy and Summer, who had been collecting berries, came over. "Hey, Ashley," Jeremy said, "I didn't know you had enough brain cells to build a tent!"

I frowned at Jeremy as he plopped himself into the nearest one.

The whole thing immediately collapsed. I gasped.

"Hey!" Jeremy cried out.

Summer climbed into another tent. That one fell down, too. I started to get a little worried.

"Ashley, since you're such a tent expert," Devon said, "maybe you can explain why all our tents are falling down."

"I'm sure it's just these two," I said, starting to put one tent back together.

Before I could fix it, Maleko came over and surveyed the damage. "What's going on?" he asked.

"We're having a problem with our job," Hans said slowly.

"What's the problem?" Maleko asked.

"Ashley made us do everything *her* way," Devon said, "and now our tents are falling down."

My mouth fell open. "It's not that I didn't listen," I said. "I just wanted to do things the *right* way."

Maleko kneeled down and inspected each tent. "You guys made a big mistake here," he said after a moment. "None of these tents will hold up. Didn't you know that the red dots on the end of the poles are supposed to match up with each other?"

Oops, I thought. *I guess I was wrong about that.* I could feel Hans and Devon staring at me.

"Does this mean we have to sleep at the hotel tonight?" Summer asked. She glanced at her sandals. "Because I could really use a pedicure!"

Maleko stood up and shook his head. "We're staying right here." He looked at Hans and Devon. "Okay. Let's take down these tents and start over. Otherwise we're all sleeping out in the open tonight."

I felt awful. Hans and Devon had been right. "I'm sorry," I said to Hans and Devon. "I should have listened to your ideas. I promise, this time, we'll build the tents however you want to do it."

"Wait a second, Ashley," Maleko said. "You don't have to rebuild the tents."

I was confused. "Why not?" I asked.

Maleko folded his arms. "You broke rule number one. You weren't a good team player. And I told you what happens if you break the rules."

I gulped. "But—" I started.

"Sorry, Ashley," Maleko said. "You're out of Wild Hawaii."

Chapter 3

Monday

Dear Diary,

Last night was the loneliest night of my life! I sat in the hotel all by myself wishing I was back at Wild Hawaii. Ms. Clare and Mr. Turnbull had rooms on the same floor as me, but they don't really count as someone to hang out with.

This morning I wandered down to the pool to catch some rays. The hotel staff here is pretty cool. They are nice and friendly and will even bring you a smoothie if you ask. I might enjoy it here if I wasn't feeling so bad for getting kicked out of the game!

"Hi, Ashley," Ms. Clare said, sitting down on the lounge chair next to mine. She was decked out in vacation gear—a tennis dress, a white floppy hat, and sneakers. "Are you having a nice day?"

I shook my head sadly. "Not really," I said. "I can't believe I'm not going back to Wild Hawaii."

Ms. Clare patted me on the arm. "Don't worry," she said. "You and I can explore lots of interesting places. We'll go anywhere you want to visit."

I smiled. "Thanks," I replied. "That sounds

21

great." But inside I was still sad. I liked Ms. Clare and all, but I wanted to spend my vacation with my friends!

Ms. Clare seemed to read my mind. "Don't forget, Ashley," she went on, "if *you* were sent back to the hotel, there *is* a chance that other students will get sent back, too. Then we can all have fun together!"

My smile got a little brighter. Ms. Clare was right. I might have a friend to hang out with sooner or later. I just hoped it was *sooner*!

Dear Diary,

I'm so bummed out about Ashley not being in the game anymore. I can't believe she was kicked out! I hope she's not too miserable back at the hotel.

This is our second night at camp. Last night everyone feasted on the fish that Campbell and I caught.

I have to say, Diary, it was the best fish I had ever tasted! There's just something about eating food you catch yourself, you know?

After dinner, we all helped clean up. Then we sat around the campfire while Maleko pointed out the constellations. It seemed like there were a million stars in the sky. Is it my imagination, or does the sky

 seem a lot bigger when you're camping out on a beach in Hawaii?

This morning we were all awake at the crack of dawn. I could have slept a lot longer, but Maleko was already up yelling, "Okay, people, let's go, let's go, *LET'S GO!*"

I staggered out of my tent and down to the beach. I washed my face with a little bowl of cold water. Freshwater is hard to come by. We collect only a certain amount from a freshwater spring each day. Just between you and me, Diary, I really miss indoor plumbing!

Phoebe snuck up on me and tried to videotape me just as I started brushing my teeth.

"Go away!" I yelled at her, although it sounded like "Ro raway!" since my toothbrush was hanging out of my mouth.

Then it was time to start our jobs for the day. I met Campbell down at our boat.

"I have an idea that will help us catch more fish," Campbell said. "I read about it in one of our books. Instead of using worms for bait, we can use little fish. We might be able to catch more big fish that way."

"Excellent thinking," I said. "I read that big fish really like to eat minnows."

"Those are the little silver ones, right?" Campbell asked.

I nodded. "Minnows hang out in shallow pools of water. We can scoop them up in buckets."

"Mary-Kate, I am so glad you're my partner," Campbell said.

Diary, I'm so glad Campbell is my partner, too! Her idea worked really well. We caught twice as many fish as yesterday. I can't believe it—just a few days ago, my idea of fishing was ordering the fried seafood special in the dining hall!

Campbell and I got a round of applause at dinner for bringing back so much food. Even Dana complimented us. I was really surprised. She never gives out compliments—unless she's talking about herself!

"We're having berries and coconuts for dessert," Summer said, as everyone finished eating. "Jeremy collected the coconuts."

Grant turned to Jeremy. "Bring them on!" he said.

Jeremy tapped a finger against his lip. "Coconuts . . . now where did I put the coconuts?"

Summer glared at him. "Jeremy! You *did* collect the coconuts, right?"

"Of course I did," Jeremy said, folding his arms. "But then they kind of . . . disappeared."

"How did that happen?" Maleko asked.

Jeremy shrugged. "I think it happened right around the time when I . . . ate them."

I gasped. "Jeremy, how could you?" I asked. Then I remembered that if there is one thing in life Jeremy can't resist, it's food!

Maleko was *not* happy. "Jeremy, you and I need to have a little talk," he said, standing up.

Jeremy followed Maleko into his tent. A few minutes later Maleko joined the group again—but Jeremy didn't.

"Okay, troops," Maleko said. "I have a surprise for you. Tomorrow we're going on a special hike."

I perked up. "Where are you taking us?" I asked.

Maleko smiled. "It's a secret. But I promise, it will be like nothing you've ever seen before!"

Everyone started buzzing excitedly. Where could we be going?

Dear Diary,

My wish has come true! Ms. Clare just told me that someone else got kicked out of Wild Hawaii. She wasn't sure who it was, though.

But it doesn't matter as long as I have company! I can't wait. We can hang out at the pool together and go to the beach. . . .

Someone knocked loudly on my door. I jumped off the bed and rushed over to answer it.

Who would it be? Mary-Kate? Julia? Seth? Grant?

I grabbed the handle and pulled open the door.

"Yo, Ashley. Got any food?" My cousin pushed past me into the room. I stared at him open-mouthed as he flopped onto my bed and grabbed the remote control.

Let's back up a second. Did I say it *didn't* matter who it was?

Well, I was wrong!

Of all people, why, oh, why, did I have to get stuck with Jeremy?

Chapter 4

Tuesday

Dear Diary,

Maleko kept us in suspense the whole morning.

"Are we going to see a waterfall?" Devon asked.

"Are we going to pick flowers?" Elise guessed.

"Are we going to a restaurant?" Summer chimed in. I think she is really starting to miss the hotel!

Maleko spread out his arms and grinned. "Way better than that. We're going to visit a volcano!"

Campbell and I jumped up and down. This was going to be so exciting!

"The name of the volcano is Kilauea," Maleko said as we began our hike. "It has several craters attached to it that are made from cooled lava."

"Excellent!" Hans said.

"The crater we're going to is called Pu'u Huluhulu," Maleko went on.

I laughed. "Try saying that three times fast."

Phoebe videotaped us marching down a narrow, muddy trail that led us to Pu'u Huluhulu. Along the way, we saw all sorts of plants with weird names like *akala* and *iliau*.

It took us an hour or so to get to the volcano. (It was so far away that we cheated a little and took a bus part of the way.) But once we were there, I couldn't believe my eyes! The ground was hard and black from lava that had dried up years ago.

"Take a look at this," Maleko said, stepping up to the edge of the crater. We followed behind him.

"Wow!" I cried. Right in front of us was a real live volcano! I could see small patches of red-yellow lava coming out of it.

"Can we hike over there?" Grant asked, taking a step forward.

Maleko put a hand on Grant's shoulder and pulled him back. "I don't think so," he said. "That lava is over two thousand degrees. You don't want to get much closer than this. But there are lots of other things we can see from right here."

"What is this?" Dana asked, pointing to a big black thing that looked like a sculpture sticking out of the ground.

"That's a lava tree," Maleko explained. "Years ago, when hot lava flowed past here, it made a cast around the tree and dried. In fact, there are lava trees all over the area."

"What about those craters over there?" Seth asked, pointing to a few deep holes that surrounded the volcano. "What are they called?"

Maleko looked out across the cavern. "Well, that one to the left is called Halema'uma'u," he said. "It's very special because the natives believe that the ancient fire goddess, Pele, lives inside."

Campbell wrinkled her nose. "Ancient fire goddess?" she repeated.

Maleko waved us into a tighter circle. "Pele is a very powerful goddess," he said. "Legend says that when she gets angry, she makes the volcano erupt."

"Has anyone ever seen her?" Hans asked.

"Some people say they have," Maleko said. "But no one knows for sure if she exists."

Come on, I thought. It was a cool story and all, but I didn't believe in fire goddesses.

Maleko talked a little more about the history of the area. Phoebe stood up with her camera and began taping the landscape. Soon Maleko decided it was time to head back to camp.

"Hey, Mary-Kate," Campbell said. "Why don't we take a souvenir?" She held up a piece of volcanic rock.

"Why didn't I think of that?" I said. I picked up my own piece of rock and took an extra one for Ashley. I knew it wasn't the same as being on the hike with us, but I thought it might cheer her up a little.

When we returned to camp, Campbell and I sat under a palm tree and checked out our souvenirs.

Maleko walked over to us. "What have you got there?" he asked.

"We took some of the volcano home with us," Campbell explained. "Cool, right?"

Maleko's eyes widened. "Oh, no," he said.

"Oh, no, what?" I asked.

Maleko sat down next to us under the tree. "I can't believe I didn't tell you the most important part of the legend of Pele," he said.

Campbell and I glanced at each other. "What is it?" she asked.

"Well, the legend says that if you take a piece of Pele's volcano, you must leave a gift in exchange," Maleko explained. "Otherwise you will be cursed. You will have horrible luck—forever!"

I breathed a sigh of relief. I thought he was going to tell us something serious! "You don't really believe that stuff, do you?" I asked.

"Yeah, those legends are just superstition,"

Campbell added. "It said so in my guidebook."

Maleko shrugged. "Many people have experienced the anger of Pele when they took something of hers and didn't leave a gift behind," he said.

Maleko seemed so serious, I almost laughed. "Well . . . thanks for the warning," I said. But I agreed with Campbell. There is no such thing as an ancient curse.

Dear Diary,

Auuuuggghhhhh! I thought getting kicked out of Wild Hawaii was bad. But being stuck at the hotel with Jeremy is much, much worse.

This morning he ate my breakfast right off my plate. Then he took my postcards. But the worst was when I was sitting by the pool, catching some rays. "Hey, Ashley, check it out!"

I glanced up from my magazine. Jeremy was standing on the diving board, waving like mad. He was wearing a green bathing suit with yellow smiley faces all over it.

"Cowabunga!" Jeremy shouted. He jumped off the diving board and curled himself into a ball.

Splash! A huge wave sprayed all over me.

Jeremy surfaced and pointed at me. "Good one, huh?" He laughed. "And that wasn't even my biggest wave!"

I looked around for Ms. Clare to see if she was watching. But she was on the tennis courts nearby playing doubles with some people from Boise, Idaho, that she had met at breakfast. She kept hitting the ball out of the court and cracking up.

Time to leave, I thought. I grabbed my sarong and my soaking-wet magazine and made a run for it.

I missed everyone at Wild Hawaii so much. What were they doing? Were they having fun? Did they miss me as much as I missed them?

I decided to sneak over there and find out. I bought a double strawberry ice cream cone at the hotel café for the trip. Then I headed outside and started down the trail that led to the camp.

I hid behind some bushes as I got closer to camp. I didn't want to run into Maleko. I was still feeling a little embarrassed that I was the first one kicked out of Wild Hawaii.

I could see the tops of the tents through the bushes. Then I heard voices. It was Summer and Elise! They were walking toward me.

"Did you notice all that seaweed just lying

around on the beach?" Summer said. "We could collect it and wrap ourselves up in it."

"Why would we want to wrap ourselves in all that slime?" Elise asked.

"My mom gets seaweed wraps at a spa and they are really expensive," Summer explained. "But we would be getting one for free!"

I stepped out from behind a tree. "Hey, guys," I whispered.

"Ashley!" Summer and Elise ran over and gave me big hugs.

"What are you doing here?" Elise asked.

"I just wanted to visit," I replied. "Is Maleko around?"

"No. Everyone else went swimming," Summer said. "They're all down by the beach."

Elise's eyes grew big. "Wow, an ice cream cone."

Summer licked her lips. "It looks so delicious."

"Want some?" I offered, holding out the cone.

"Sure!" Summer and Elise said at the same time. Diary, I don't think I have ever seen two people eat ice cream so fast!

"It must be nice on the outside." Elise's shoulders slumped.

"It's okay," I replied, shrugging. I told them all about the pool and the smoothies and the TV with one hundred and twenty channels.

"I wish I was back at the hotel with you, Ashley," Summer said wistfully.

"Me, too!" Elise agreed. "This roughing-it thing is cool—but sipping smoothies by the pool sounds much cooler!"

"You're lucky you got kicked out," Summer added.

"Hey, wait a minute," I said. "I have a great idea."

"No, *I* have a great idea," Elise replied.

Summer smiled. "No, I do! If Ashley had no trouble getting kicked out, then *we* shouldn't have a problem either! Right, Elise?"

"Right!" Elise said.

"Cool!" I cried. "And I know just how you can do it."

Chapter 5

Wednesday

Dear Diary,

I have a really good feeling about  today.

I'm not sure why. Maybe it's because Campbell and I keep helping out so many people with advice from our survival guide. Last night we showed Summer a new plant that grows the best-tasting fruit. We helped Grant dry firewood in record time and figured out a cool way to make our tents extra cozy. Diary, we are becoming real wilderness girls!

Campbell and I skipped down to the beach that afternoon to go fishing. As we approached the water, Campbell stopped in her tracks. "Oh, no!"

"What is it?" I asked.

And then I saw. Next to the boat our bucket of bait was lying on its side in the sand. There were no minnows left anywhere!

"How did this happen?" I cried.

Campbell groaned. "We can't collect more minnows now. The high tide probably washed all their pools away."

"Well, we still have to catch food for dinner," I

said. "So what do you think we should do?"

"Let's just dig up some worms and head out," Campbell replied.

"Okay," I agreed. "Go team!" I added, trying to keep our spirits up.

Campbell peeked inside the boat. "Um, Mary-Kate, where are our digging shells?"

I followed her gaze. "I don't know." I scratched my head. "I thought I left them right there."

Campbell sighed. "I guess we'll have to find new ones."

We spent the next ten minutes looking for big shells that were good for digging. But the only ones we could find were either broken or too small.

"Come on. We're wasting time," I said, handing Campbell a broken shell. "Let's just use these."

We dug and we dug. But for some reason, all the worms were in hiding today, because we found only ten. By the end of the day we had caught a grand total of five fish. If you want to get technical, five not very big fish.

As we trudged back to camp, the cooking crew saw us coming and cheered. "How many do you have for us today?" Dana called.

Campbell and I exchanged a glance. "Um, five," she mumbled.

"That's it?" Seth asked, looking inside our bucket.

I quickly made up an excuse. "There were bad fishing conditions today," I said. "It was, uh, too sunny."

"Too sunny?" Elise echoed.

"Yeah," I went on. "Our survival guide said that some fish don't like too much sun."

Okay, so our book never told us that. But I had to say something, Diary!

"This isn't enough food," Seth grumbled. "Everyone is going to be hungry."

I stared down at the sand. I didn't want anyone to be disappointed with us.

"Don't worry, guys," Dana said. "I know this recipe my mom and dad make a lot. If I mix some coconut and coconut juice in with the fish and make this stew-y stuff out of it, it will seem like a lot more food."

I couldn't believe that she was being so nice about the whole thing. Dana, of all people!

The stew turned out to be really delicious. But I had a hard time enjoying it. Right before dinner Campbell and I overheard some people talking about us.

"They were probably goofing off instead of

catching fish," Seth grumbled to Julia.

"Maybe they think because they caught a bunch of fish yesterday, they can slack off," Julia suggested.

"Do you think Maleko is going to send them back to the hotel, just like Ashley and Jeremy?" Hans asked.

I gasped. The situation wasn't that serious, was it?

"Don't worry," Campbell whispered to me. "We did really well yesterday and the day before. Tomorrow will be fine."

"You're probably right," I said, feeling a little better. "Anyone can have a bad day."

In fact, the group kind of forgot about the fish when Summer announced that there would be no berries for dessert.

"No dessert?" Hans cried. "Why not?"

"I gave myself a berry facial before dinner," Summer explained, "and before I knew it I used up all the berries. Sorry!"

She didn't seem too sorry, though. She wasn't even upset when Maleko told her that she had broken the rules and would have to leave.

You know what else, Diary? I

might have been imagining it—but I could swear I saw Summer give Elise a high five when she left to go back to the hotel. What's up with *that*?

Dear Diary,

"Ashley, check out this top! And look at this! Have you ever seen such a beautiful sundress before?"

Summer was speed-reading through a pile of teen magazines. You would think she hadn't seen a fashion magazine in years and years.

We were lounging in the hotel hot tub. There was a full moon in the sky, the air was really warm, and the best part was, Jeremy wasn't around!

"Why didn't I think of this before?" Summer asked, putting down a magazine. She picked up her smoothie and raised it in the air. "I owe my freedom to you, Ashley. Thanks for the berry facial idea!"

I raised my smoothie, too. "And tomorrow night, if Elise does what she's supposed to do, she'll be free, too!"

We clinked cups. Life was very, very good.

Chapter 6

Thursday

Dear Diary,

I never should have gotten up today, because everything went wrong! It all started after breakfast.

"Campbell," I said, as we all finished eating, "since the cooking crew covered for us yesterday, why don't we offer to clean up breakfast for them?"

"Sounds good to me," Campbell said.

"Can Campbell and I clean up for you?" I asked Seth, Dana, and Elise. "You know, to thank you for helping us out with dinner yesterday."

"Sure!" Dana said.

"That would be awesome," Seth added.

"Yeah, thanks, you guys," Elise chimed in.

Dana, Elise, and Seth walked off as Campbell and I started to throw paper plates into a garbage bag.

I nodded and waved to them. "This shouldn't take too long," I said to Campbell as I threw away a mango pit.

I was right. A few minutes later we had packed everything into the garbage bag.

"Make sure you tie the bag tightly," Campbell said. "It's pretty breezy."

"No problem," I said, and twisted the top of the bag into a knot.

"Finished!" Campbell exclaimed. "Time to go swimming!"

We had the best time swimming in the lagoon with some of the other kids. But when Campbell and I came back a few hours later—

"Oh, no!" I gasped. Garbage was scattered all over the sand. And our bag was wide open!

"Mary-Kate, I told you to tie the bag tightly," Campbell complained.

"I did!" I cried. "At least I thought I did."

Campbell sighed. "Well, we'd better clean up this trash before Maleko sees it."

But we were too late. Seth, Dana, Elise, and Maleko walked up to us.

"What happened here?" Maleko asked, surveying the mess.

"We told the cooking crew we would clean up for them." I groaned. "But I guess we didn't tie the garbage bag good enough."

"We're really sorry," Campbell said.

"We'll clean it up right now," I added.

"I'll help," Dana offered. "Then we'll finish faster."

"That's the spirit!" Maleko said.

Seth and Elise slowly joined in. But I was pretty

sure they weren't happy that they had to do it.

"So much for being helpful," Campbell muttered as we started picking up the garbage again.

"No kidding," I said. "We'll definitely have to catch extra fish to make up for this one. Let's start early today."

"Sounds good to me," Campbell said.

A half hour later we headed over to the boat.

"Boy, these past two days haven't been much fun," Campbell said.

"Tell me about it," I said. "First our bait and digging shells disappear. Then we mess up garbage duty."

"Campbell," I said slowly, "I know this is going to sound weird, but do you think all this bad luck we've been having has anything to do with the curse of Pele?"

"You mean if we don't leave her a gift we'll have bad luck forever?" Campbell snorted. "Give me a break, Mary-Kate. We just had a bad morning, that's all."

I took a deep breath. Campbell was probably right. I mean, I didn't believe in the legend before, so why should I believe it now? So what if we had a little bad luck. It was just a coincidence.

We climbed into the rowboat. "Okay, let's make a

pact that all bad luck ends right now," I said.

"Agreed," Campbell said. She glanced around the inside of the boat. "Uh, MK? Did you do something with the oars?"

I shook my head. "No. Why?"

"Because they're not here," Campbell said.

I scanned the nearby beach. There was no sign of the oars there either. Where could they have gone? I looked out into the lagoon.

That's when I saw them. They were floating way out in the water. "Campbell, look!" I cried.

"How did they fall out of the rowboat?" Campbell asked.

"I don't know, but we have to go after them," I replied. "Let's paddle ourselves out there with our hands."

"Isn't that going to be hard?" Campbell asked.

"We'll find out," I said as I started paddling.

"I feel like my arms are about to fall off," Campbell grumbled after a few minutes.

"Me, too," I panted. "But we can do it." I leaned over the side of the boat. "Paddle harder!"

Then I realized Campbell was leaning over the same side of the boat as I was.

"Maybe you should paddle on the other side," I pointed out. "We don't want to—"

Too late. The rowboat tipped over and we fell right into the water.

I bobbed under the waves and then surfaced and spit out some salt water. Campbell popped up next to me.

"Oh, no!" She groaned. "Phoebe is taping us from the beach!"

I looked over. Phoebe put down her camera and waved at us as she walked away.

"Great," I said. "Plus our rowboat is upside down." I nodded toward the boat floating nearby.

I swam a few strokes closer to rescue it. "What's all this slimy brown stuff in the water?" I asked, swimming through it.

"Mary-Kate, it's our bait!" Campbell cried. "It's getting in your hair."

"Eeewwww!" I shrieked. I dove under the water and shook my head. Then I swam away as quickly as I could.

Campbell managed to flip the rowboat and climb back in. I swam over and climbed in, too. Then we paddled slowly to shore and dragged ourselves onto the beach.

"I have a feeling we're not going to catch many

fish today." Campbell plopped down onto the sand.

"Tell me about it," I said, sitting next to her. "I'm really beginning to think Maleko was right. Maybe we *are* cursed!"

Campbell let some sand trickle through her fingers. "Mary-Kate, that's stupid," she said. "There is no way we're having all this bad luck just because we didn't leave Pele a gift."

But I didn't think it was stupid. This was just too much of a coincidence for me.

"Hey," Dana called. "Are you guys taking a break?" She was walking toward us, carrying a basket of berries.

"Hey, Dana," I mumbled.

Dana stopped and gave us a once-over. "Why are you all wet?" she asked.

"We fell out of the rowboat," Campbell explained in a low voice. I braced myself for an insult.

"Want some berries?" Dana asked. "I'm making them into a soup for dinner tonight."

My eyebrows shot up. Was that all she was going to say?

"Uh, thanks," I replied. I took a handful and popped one in my mouth. It was delicious.

"So what's going on?" Dana asked, putting down her basket.

"We kind of had an accident," Campbell explained.

"What happened?" Dana asked, sounding concerned. "Are you okay?"

It was so weird. I mean, she really seemed to care. I decided to spill the story.

"And if we don't catch any fish today, we'll probably get kicked out of the game," Campbell added when I was done.

"Don't worry. You won't get kicked out." Dana smiled. "Hey, I don't have cooking duty for a few more hours. Maybe I can help you catch some fish."

Why is Dana being so nice to us? I wondered. Then I realized that she probably was just doing it because she wanted to win the gift certificate.

In any case, I was glad Dana helped us out. Within a few hours Campbell, Dana, and I had caught a ton of fish! We brought them to Seth and Elise so they could start cooking dinner.

"Elise, can I have some water?" Seth asked, holding out his hand.

"Oh, yeah," Elise said, examining her fingernails. "About the water. We don't have any."

"Weren't you supposed to collect it today?" Dana asked.

"Mmm-hmm." Elise shrugged. "But I used it all for something really important."

"What?" Seth asked.

"My hair," Elise replied. She flipped her long brown hair back and forth. "Doesn't it look better now that I washed it?"

I stared openmouthed at Elise. This didn't seem like her at all. She was usually super-responsible.

I'm sure you know what happened next. Elise got kicked out of the game! At least Ashley will have one more person to hang out with.

Everyone was happy with us again at dinner. I expected Dana to stand up and say that she helped us catch the fish, but she didn't say anything. Didn't she want to show off her good teamwork? Why would she help us if she didn't want the credit?

Is it possible that she was just being . . . nice?

Dear Diary,

"Is that the Glittery Grape? Pass it over, will you?"

"Who has Peppermint Pink?"

Summer, Elise, and I were giving one another pedicures in my room to celebrate Elise leaving

Wild Hawaii. Our plan totally worked!

Summer and Elise were both in super-good moods. "This is way better than picking coconuts

and berries," Summer said as she carefully painted Elise's toenails.

"Absolutely," Elise agreed. "How did I ever live without a bed?"

"I can't even remember why I was upset for getting kicked out of the game," I added. "I would much rather hang out in the hotel than rough it in a tent on the beach."

"So what should we do tomorrow?" Summer leaned back on a pillow.

Her question gave me an idea. One that I was sure would make my friends even happier!

"Girls, tomorrow is going to be our most fun day yet," I said. "I'm going to have a sleepover in my room to celebrate our freedom."

"Excellent!" Elise gave me a high five. "It's party time!"

Chapter 7

Friday

Dear Diary,

This morning, Campbell and I offered to collect berries for breakfast. I guess we were hoping to make up for the garbage incident yesterday.

"So what do you want to do on our day off tomorrow?" I asked as we strolled up to the campsite with two full buckets of berries.

"Why don't we go exploring?" Campbell suggested. She plunked down her bucket next to the camp's cooking supplies.

I hesitated. "I'm not sure I want to," I said, placing my bucket next to hers.

"Why not?" Campbell asked.

"Because think of all the bad luck we might have if we did that!" I said. "We could get lost, or get trapped in a cave, or something."

Campbell laughed. "Come on, Mary-Kate," she said. "Nothing else is going to happen to us."

Famous last words, right, Diary? Because when we came back an hour later, the cooking crew was busy making breakfast. And they weren't happy to see us!

"You could have picked more than ten berries,"

Seth pointed out as soon as soon as we walked up.

"What do you mean?" I asked. "We brought you two full buckets."

"The buckets weren't full when we got here," Elise said.

"I don't get it," Campbell said.

"What's going on, gang?" Maleko asked, strolling over to our group.

"Uh, well, we accidentally messed up breakfast," I admitted. I explained the situation.

"Wait a second," Dana said. "Maybe some birds came and ate the berries. That's possible, right?"

"But no birds ever ate any of the food we left out before," Elise said.

"That's because nobody else has our bad luck," I muttered to Campbell. "I told you it wasn't over."

"Bad luck?" Maleko asked. "I warned you, didn't I?" he said, wagging a finger at me.

"Tell me about it," I said as Maleko walked away.

I turned to Campbell. "I think Maleko is right," I said. "Pele is mad because we didn't leave her a gift."

Campbell stared at me in amazement. "Mary-Kate, are you kidding me?"

"I know it sounds weird," I answered, "but how else can you explain all our horrible luck?"

Campbell shrugged. "I don't know. But I'm

pretty sure it has nothing to do with a goddess that lives in a volcano."

"Just to be on the safe side," I said, "how about we hike back to the volcano tomorrow and leave Pele some presents?"

Campbell rolled her eyes. "Oh, all right. If you really want to. Just let me know when we're leaving."

I smiled. I felt better knowing we were going back. I mean, deep down I didn't *really* believe in the curse of Pele. (But just to be on the safe side, I wouldn't mind visiting the volcano again.)

Dear Diary,

Summer, Elise, and I had the best time in my room tonight. Summer borrowed a boom box from the front desk so we could play our 4-You CDs. Elise brought all her makeup along so we could give one another makeovers.

Best of all, we knew Jeremy wouldn't crash our party because he was busy watching *Revenge of the Killer Mummies Part Two: Terror in Texas* on cable.

I sat in a chair and studied the room-service menu.

"Check it out, guys," I said, flipping through the

plastic-coated pages. "We can order ten kinds of ice cream in one big bowl!"

Summer turned up the 4-You song that was playing on the radio and bopped over to the chair. "Sounds good to me," she said. "While you're at it, can you order me some cheese fries?"

"And I wouldn't mind some veggies and dip," Elise added.

"Let's rent a movie, too!" Summer suggested. "You can do that just by using the remote control." She pressed some buttons on the TV remote and a really good movie appeared on the screen.

I picked up the phone and gave the man at the front desk our order. I added a few more things from the menu, just in case we were still hungry later on. The man promised to have our food delivered within an hour.

"An hour!" Summer cried. "All this talk about food has made me seriously hungry."

"Me, too," I agreed. My eyes landed on the minifridge underneath the TV. "Hey, what's in there?" I asked.

I peeked inside. "All right!" I cheered. The fridge was stocked with juice, soda, and snacks. Before we knew it, the three of us had eaten it all.

Diary, our party was a blast. We watched the movie, danced, sang, and ate until we were stuffed. It was the greatest night ever!

Ring! Ring!
The next morning I woke up  to the sound of the phone jangling next to my ear on the night table. *Who could be calling me this early?* I wondered. I reached over and picked it up. "Hello?"

"Hello. This is Mr. Kawabata," the voice on the other end of the line said. "I'm the hotel manager."

"Who is it?" Elise called from the next bed. I waved my hand for her to be quiet.

"How can I help you?" I asked in my most polite voice.

"I'm sorry to bother you," Mr. Kawabata said, "but I was going through my computer records and saw that you made a lot of room service charges last night. A few hundred dollars' worth, in fact."

"Um, I guess we were really hungry," I said, not sure what else to say. *Why is he calling to tell me this?* I wondered.

Mr. Kawabata cleared his throat. "I'm not sure

your chaperons, Mr. Turnbull and Ms. Clare, made it clear to you. But room service is not part of your vacation package."

"What?" I gulped. Then I had an even worse thought. "How about the minifridge? Is that included?"

"No, I'm afraid it's not," Mr. Kawabata replied. "I'm calling to make sure you will be able to pay the bill."

I almost dropped the phone. There was *no way* we could pay for all the food we ate.

Which meant one thing. We were in big trouble!

Chapter 8

Saturday

Dear Diary,

Elise, Summer, and I spent the rest  of the morning trying to come up with ways to get the money for our room-service bill without Ms. Clare or Mr. Turnbull finding out.

"What are we going to do!" Summer wailed, flopping over on my bed.

Elise hugged a pillow. "If Ms. Clare and Mr. Turnbull find out what we did, we are toast," she added.

"I'm pretty sure our parents won't be too happy with us either," Summer said.

"We have to talk to the manager," I said. "Maybe if we promise we'll never order room service again, he will forget the whole thing."

I didn't believe that one myself, but I was trying to look on the bright side.

I could tell Elise and Summer weren't thrilled with the thought of talking to the manager of the hotel. But what else could we do?

The three of us went downstairs and found Mr. Kawabata's office. I took a deep breath, plastered on my biggest smile, and marched in.

"Good morning, ladies," Mr. Kawabata said, looking up from his desk. "How can I help you?"

"I'm Ashley Burke," I said. "We spoke on the phone this morning."

"Ah, yes, Ms. Burke." Mr. Kawabata shook my hand with an amused smile. "You must be here to discuss your food charges."

"Um, sort of." I looked at Elise and Summer for support, but they seemed ready to run out the door at any second. Then I turned back to Mr. Kawabata. "Um, we don't really have the money to pay our bill," I told him.

"I see," Mr. Kawabata said. "I'm sure your chaperons can settle the bill for now." He picked up the phone.

"Please, Mr. Kawabata. Ms. Clare and Mr. Turnbull can't find out about this," I said. "They'll tell our parents and we'll get in really big trouble!"

"It was a huge mistake," Elise added. "We'll never do it again."

"We promise!" Summer chimed in.

"I'm sorry," Mr. Kawabata said. "But I have no other choice. Your bill has to be settled somehow."

He started to dial the phone.

I glanced around desperately, hoping an answer would fall out of the air. I noticed a cleaning lady pushing her cart past the doorway. That gave me an idea. "Wait!" I cried. "What if we worked at the hotel to pay off our bill?"

Mr. Kawabata hung up the phone. "Hmmm," he said slowly. "I suppose I *could* give you some odd jobs around the hotel. Are you sure you're willing to do that?"

"Definitely," I said. I turned to Elise and Summer. "Right, guys?"

"R-right," Elise and Summer said together. They didn't look as sure as I felt, though.

"Okay then," Mr. Kawabata said.

"Guys, isn't that great?" I asked as we left the manager's office.

"Yeah, terrific," Elise grumbled.

"It's just how I wanted to spend my vacation," Summer added.

"Come on," I said. "So we answer some telephones and make some beds for the next few days. It won't be so bad. Really."

Dear Diary,

This morning I woke up bright and  early to hike to the volcano. I headed over to Campbell's tent to wake her up. I met Dana on the way.

"Hi, Mary-Kate," she said. "What are you doing out so early?"

"Campbell and I are going back to the volcano today to leave Pele some gifts," I explained.

"Cool," Dana said. "Do you mind if I come with you?"

I thought about it for a second. Dana wasn't so bad to be around these days. "Why not?" I replied. "We can all go together. I'm just going to wake up Campbell now."

"Oh, I'll get her," Dana said, heading toward Campbell's tent. "That way you can get ready. I'm all set to go."

"Thanks, Dana." I smiled and went back to my tent. Wow. Maybe the Wild Hawaii experience really did bring out the best in people. It sure was working on Dana.

Dana peeked into my tent a few minutes later. She was alone. Her mouth was set in a tight line. "I talked to Campbell about the hike," she said.

"Is she getting ready?" I asked.

"Campbell isn't coming. She said . . ." Dana's voice drifted off.

"What?" I asked. "What did she say?"

"Nothing. Never mind." Dana looked down.

What is it that she doesn't want to tell me? I wondered. "Dana, what did she say?" I repeated.

"Okay, okay." Dana took a deep breath. "Campbell said that you are totally out of control with this whole Pele thing. She's never seen you act so dumb."

I shook my head. "No way," I replied. "Campbell would never say that about me."

"Whatever, Mary-Kate," Dana said. "But that's what she told me."

I was so confused. I know Campbell didn't believe in the legend of Pele. But why would she say such mean things about me? And why would she bail on our plans?

I'll talk to her later, I decided.

"I guess it's just us then," I said, picking up my backpack.

Mr. Turnbull had agreed to come along on our hike to make sure we were okay. Today he was dressed in khaki shorts, orange socks, hiking boots, and a T-shirt that said I LOVE HAWAII. He was carrying huge binoculars.

I wanted to get to the volcano as fast as possible. But Mr. Turnbull kept slowing us down. Every few  feet he wanted to stop and study plants and insects. With each stop he would say things like "Excellent specimen of orchid!" or "Superb bromeliad!" Dana and I just rolled our eyes at each other and giggled.

SUPERB BROMELIAD

Along the way Dana and I talked. And talked. And talked. Back at school we never had a real conversation. She definitely seemed different now that we were in Hawaii. And you know what, Diary? I almost like her.

"I can't believe Campbell said you were dumb," Dana commented as we approached the base of the volcano. "Best friends shouldn't talk that way about each other. I know *I* wouldn't talk about my best friend that way."

I shrugged. I didn't want to say anything bad about Campbell. But deep down I felt a pang. Dana was right. Best friends *shouldn't* talk that way about each other.

"I hate to say it, Mary-Kate, but I guess you're just nicer than Campbell is," Dana went on.

I didn't know what to say to that. And I really

didn't want to talk about this anymore. "Hey, that's where we found those rocks." I pointed up ahead.

"Let's go," Dana said.

We left Mr. Turnbull behind to inspect some dried lava.

I took off my backpack and opened it. I had no idea what kind of gifts Pele would want so I had brought along a paper clip, a pink barrette, and a coconut. I figured she would have to like one of them!

I knelt down and laid the gifts on the ground. "There. Do you think my bad luck will go away now?" I asked Dana.

"I'm sure of it!" Dana said, nodding. "Hmm . . . wait a sec, I'll be right back."

She wandered off and returned a few minutes later with a handful of colorful flowers. She put them down on top of my gifts. "There," she said, "now it's perfect. Pele is sure to get over her grumpy mood when she sees these!"

I laughed. "Come on, we'd better get back," I said. "It's almost time to start our chores."

We headed down the trail, picking up Mr. Turnbull along the way. It was a breezy day. Big colorful birds swooped down over us as we hiked. I felt as if a huge weight had lifted off my shoulders.

 I could tell—my luck was beginning to change already!

"I'm so glad we went to the volcano," I told Dana as we neared the camp. "Thanks for coming with me."

"No problem," Dana said, grinning. "After all, what are friends for?"

Friends? Me and Dana Woletsky? A week ago I wouldn't have thought that was possible.

But maybe I just didn't know the real Dana, Diary.

Chapter 9

Sunday

Dear Diary,

How bad could working in the hotel be? I'll tell you how bad it could be! Worse than I ever thought!

"Where are the Band-Aids?" Summer asked as she ran past me at the pool.

I peeked out from behind the enormous tray of food I was carrying. "In the white cabinet. Do you remember if we have guava smoothies on the menu?" I asked. "The lady at table five wants one."

"I'm not sure," Summer replied. "We have ten kinds. Mango . . . and, uh, nine other ones."

"Oh, well. I'll figure it out." I turned around and knocked right into Elise, who was speeding the other way.

Crash! My tray fell to the floor.

"Oh, no!" I cried.

"If people need chips and salsa so badly, why can't they get up and get it themselves?" Elise cried. "I'm busy!"

Uh-oh, I thought. *She has totally lost it.*

"Is there a problem?" Mr. Kawabata asked, walking over to us.

"No problem at all," I said, quickly piling the dishes back onto the tray.

"Good," he replied. "Because those people on the lounge chairs would like a pineapple smoothie, table three needs their lunch order, and the lifeguards are asking for more sunscreen."

Elise, Summer, and I all sighed at the same time. Then we took off again.

By the middle of the afternoon, the three of us had had it. We plopped down on some lounge chairs by the pool to take a break.

"This is torture," Summer complained.

"Did we have to eat *everything* in the minifridge?" Elise groaned.

"Look at it this way," I said. "At least we didn't get in trouble for anything. And our bill is already half paid."

Summer and Elise scowled at me.

I sat forward in my chair. "Okay, you're right. This is the pits. Even Wild Hawaii is better than this!"

"Do you really think so?" a voice behind me said.

I whipped around. It was Ms. Clare! She was dressed in a flowered muumuu and sandals.

"Uh-oh," I muttered. How much of our conversation had she heard?

Apparently not that much, since Ms. Clare sat down on my lounge chair and smiled at the three of us.

"I feel terrible that you girls aren't participating in Wild Hawaii anymore," she said. "And I'm sorry you don't like hanging out at the hotel."

"That's okay," I said slowly. Ms. Clare had obviously misunderstood our conversation. She thought we were saying that lounging at the hotel wasn't as fun as being in Wild Hawaii!

"No, it's not okay," Ms. Clare went on. "I'm going to make sure you girls get involved again."

"You are?" Summer asked warily.

Ms. Clare nodded. "Maleko was just saying this morning that he needed some extra help around the camp. I'll bet you three would be perfect for the job!"

A bad feeling swirled in the pit of my stomach. "Help?" I echoed. "What kind of help?"

"I'm not sure," Ms. Clare said. "But just think— you'll get to go back to camp and see all your friends again!"

"What about Jeremy?" I asked. "Is he going, too?"

Ms. Clare shook her head. "No. Jeremy seems very happy at the hotel."

"Oh," I said.

"So it's settled then," Ms. Clare said. "Starting today, you're back on part-time duty for Wild Hawaii. Come on, let's go over to the camp right now."

The three of us dragged ourselves off the lounge chairs and followed Ms. Clare to the Wild Hawaii camp.

"Nice to see you," Maleko said when we arrived at camp.

"The girls really missed Wild Hawaii," Ms. Clare explained, "so they came back to help out."

"That's the team spirit I'm looking for!" Maleko said. "Why don't you start by picking some berries? And when you're finished with that, you can refill the water bottles."

"Great," I said, smiling tightly. All I could think about was that we still had to go back to the hotel and finish our work there!

So now we have two jobs instead of one, Diary. And it's all because of me and my big mouth.

Dear Diary,

I don't know if it has anything to do with my visit to the volcano, but nothing has gone wrong all morning. I hope this is a sign for what the rest of the day is going to be like!

Today we're going to another exciting place—a three-hundred-foot waterfall! The name of the waterfall is Umauma.

As we began our hike to the beach, I started to make my way over to Campbell. I wanted to ask her why she didn't come to the volcano. But Dana grabbed my arm and asked if we could walk together.

"Um, sure," I replied. She was so nice yesterday. How could I say no?

We started gabbing about our trip to the volcano. Just as we were cracking up about Mr. Turnbull, Campbell brushed past me on the trail.

"Oh, hey, Campbell." I smiled at her. "I was looking for you before. Do you want to hang out with us?"

Campbell glanced at Dana, then at me. "No. I told Julia I'd hang with her." She walked ahead.

Was it me, Diary, or did Campbell seem really mad at me? What did I do?

"Nice talking to you, Campbell," Dana said

sarcastically. "Hey, Mary-Kate, check out that lizard over there!"

As we hiked, I kept wondering why Campbell was acting so strangly. *Maybe she is just in a bad mood or something*, I thought.

Pretty soon we reached the waterfall. Exotic birds swooped through the air.

"Those are *anianiau* and white-footed boobies," Maleko pointed out. The water tumbled over rock formations and landed in a big emerald-colored pool. There were tiny rainbows in the air from where the sunlight hit the drops of water as they fell.

I saw Campbell standing alone by the waterfall. I decided to go over and talk to her.

"Pretty cool beach, huh?" I asked.

"Whatever," Campbell said, not looking at me.

What is wrong with her? I wondered. "Soooo, when do you want to go fishing today?" I tried again.

Campbell turned her back on me completely. "Maybe you should go fishing with Dana instead," she suggested. "I don't feel like going." She walked away.

I was speechless. *What just happened here?* I thought. *First Campbell is acting all mean to me and now she doesn't want to talk to me at all?*

I guess my bad luck hasn't gone away, Diary. Because what could be worse luck than not getting along with your best friend—and not knowing why?

Chapter 10

Monday

Dear Diary,

What was Campbell's problem? I tossed and turned last night in my tent, trying to figure out why she was acting so strangely.

Well, whatever it was, I wanted to fix it as soon as possible. I wasn't sure if she would talk to me, so I decided to write her a note.

Dear Campbell,

I'm not sure why you don't want to hang out with me anymore. But if I did something to make you angry, I'm sorry! Can we talk about it and figure things out? You're my best friend.

Love,
Mary-Kate

I read it and reread it. Then I decided to leave some pretty flowers with the note.

I hiked to a spot near the

beach where lots of different-colored flowers grew. I started picking a few of them when I heard a familiar voice behind me.

"Hey, Mary-Kate!"

I turned around. It was Dana.

"Hey," I said. "What's going on?"

"Not much," she replied. "What are you doing?"

I told her about what had happened with Campbell. Then I mentioned how I wanted to leave the flowers for her, along with an apology note.

"That is so sweet," Dana said enthusiastically. "Where are you going to leave it?"

"In her tent," I said. "That way she won't miss it."

Dana nodded. "Campbell *has* to talk to you after that," she said. "Want me to help you pick some flowers?"

I never thought I'd say this, but I'm kind of glad I had Dana around. She really made me feel better. A few minutes later, I left a huge bunch of flowers on top of Campbell's sleeping bag, along with the note.

I was sure that once Campbell saw them she would forgive me.

Dear Diary,

The nightmare continues.

This morning, Summer, Elise, and I were back at the hotel, waiting on the guests at the pool. Then this afternoon we were back at camp, doing more chores. And to make things worse, Phoebe was videotaping us for her documentary the entire time we were at camp. Now everyone back at school would see us all gross and covered with dirt!

One bright spot about being at camp is that I get to see Mary-Kate. She was totally psyched when we ran into each other after lunch.

"What are you *doing* here?" she shrieked, hugging me.

I explained the whole horrible story.

"That's awful," Mary-Kate said. "But I have to tell you something even worse! Campbell doesn't want to be my friend anymore."

"What?" I exclaimed. "Did you have a huge fight with her or something?"

"Not really." Mary-Kate sighed. "She just won't talk to me. I left her a note and some flowers today, but she hasn't said anything about it."

"Maybe she just didn't see them yet," I said.

"Mary-Kate! Time to get going!" Maleko called.

"Give me an update later," I said.

Mary-Kate nodded and ran off to join the rest of the group.

I sighed and trudged down to the spring with a bucket. I felt really bad for Mary-Kate. Why would Campbell act so weird?

As I dipped the bucket into the water, I overheard a conversation coming from a nearby patch of trees. *Ooh, maybe it's some good gossip to share with Elise and Summer,* I thought. The sound of a small waterfall nearby was making it hard to hear who was talking so I leaned in to listen.

"I *thought* she was my friend, but I'm not so sure anymore," a girl's voice said.

"How come?" a second girl asked.

"You think she's loyal, but she's not what she seems."

Wow, I thought. *Whoever they're talking about sounds like bad news.*

"I never would have thought that about her," the second girl replied.

"Well, believe it," the first girl said. "Mary-Kate is not the person people think she is."

They were talking about my sister! I had to find out who it was.

I walked closer to the voices and peeked around a tree.

I blinked and blinked. I couldn't believe it. It was Julia and Campbell, sitting on a rock by the waterfall.

"I don't think I want to be her friend anymore," Campbell said.

I gasped. *Campbell* was the one talking about Mary-Kate!

Chapter 11

Tuesday

Dear Diary,

I was so upset when Ashley told me the horrible things that Campbell said about me. When I was finished being upset I started getting angry. So much that I refused to be in the same place as Campbell the entire day.

But once the afternoon rolled around, there was no getting past it—we were teammates. I had to go fishing with her.

I strolled up to the boat. Campbell was already there, putting some minnows into a bucket. My chest felt really tight. How was I going to get through this?

"I thought you didn't want to go fishing with me," I said, crossing my arms.

"I'm just trying to be a team player," Campbell said.

Then I noticed that my fishing pole wasn't where I had left it. Campbell's was right there in the boat.

"Campbell," I said. "Have you seen my fishing pole?"

"No," she replied. "Is it missing?"

"Yeah." I shrugged. *Maybe I took it back to my tent*

or something, I thought. "I'm going to find it," I said. "I'll be right back."

I trudged back to the campsite and searched my tent. Nope. No fishing pole. *Where could it be?* I wondered.

I hunted around camp a bit and then gave up. I was going to have to tell Campbell we were fishing with one pole today.

I headed back to the row-boat. On the way, I noticed something pointy sticking out of Campbell's tent.

That's weird, I thought. *It's shaped just like . . .*

I glanced around to make sure no one was watching me. Then I knelt down and unzipped the flap.

I gasped. My fishing pole was lying across Campbell's sleeping bag!

Now I was really angry. Campbell had hidden my fishing pole on purpose. Why? Because she didn't want me to go fishing with her?

"What are you doing in my tent?"

I whipped around. Campbell was standing behind me with her arms folded across her chest.

I held up my fishing pole. "Why is my fishing pole in your tent?" I asked. "You said you didn't know where it was."

Campbell's jaw dropped. "I didn't! I have no idea how it got there."

"Yeah, right," I shot back. "Then why did you come back to the campsite just now? I'll bet it was to make sure I didn't find it!"

"That's not true!" Campbell shook her head. "I was coming to help you."

I turned away from Campbell. "You're lying," I said.

"H-how can you say that?" Campbell sputtered.

I faced her again. "I can't trust anything you say these days."

Campbell's lower lip trembled. "Fine!" she shouted. "If that's what you think, then I don't want to be friends anymore!" Campbell took off running.

"Fine!" I shouted back.

But it wasn't fine. I was angry with Campbell, but the last thing I wanted was to lose my best friend.

Dear Diary,

Tomorrow is the last day of Wild Hawaii. If you ask me, the whole trip has been a major disaster in the friend-ship department. Summer, Elise, and I are not hav-ing any fun together at all. And at camp this morning Mary-Kate told me about her blow-out fight with Campbell.

Mary-Kate was really upset. "I just don't know how this happened," she said in a shaky voice as we sat together on the beach. "Campbell said she hadn't seen my fishing pole, but there it was—sticking out of her tent!"

"That doesn't sound like Campbell at all," I said. Then I thought back to the nasty things I had heard Campbell say about Mary-Kate.

"You wouldn't believe it, Ashley," Mary-Kate said, "but the person who has been helping me through this, besides you, is Dana!"

"Dana who?" I asked. There was no way my sister was talking about Dana Woletsky!

"I know it sounds crazy," Mary-Kate said, "but Dana and I are kind of friends now."

"How did that happen?" I asked.

Mary-Kate shrugged. "I'm not really sure. All I know is that she's not the person we thought she was. I bet you would like her, too, if you got to know her."

"I'm not so sure about that one," I pointed out. "What about the time she tried to steal my boyfriend, Ross? Or when she tried to lose that sports tournament in Florida just because I was team captain? She's really mean, Mary-Kate."

"I know, but she's different now," Mary-Kate explained. "I think Wild Hawaii really changed her."

"Ummmm, if you say so," I said. But secretly there was no way I believed Dana could be that different.

Mary-Kate sighed. "But I don't want to talk about Dana. I want to talk about Campbell. Do you think she is telling the truth?" Mary-Kate asked.

"I don't know," I said. "We need to find out what's really going on around here."

"How?" Mary-Kate asked, sniffling.

I stood up and brushed some sand off my shorts. "When I'm done working here, I'll do a little snooping around and see what I can find out."

"Thanks, Ashley," Mary-Kate replied. "You are the greatest sister in the world!"

I grinned. "I know, I know." I was happy to help out Mary-Kate. That's what sisters are for!

I stifled a yawn as I helped Mary-Kate to her feet. Diary, I'm probably the only person ever to come to Hawaii on vacation—and end up working as a waitress, dishwasher, towel girl, and spy!

Chapter 12

Thursday

Dear Diary,

This is the last day of our Wild  Hawaii adventure. I'm not exactly sure when it got this bad—but teamwork has reached an all-time low.

Campbell and I decided to fish at different times during the day, so we wouldn't have to see each other. Once everyone else noticed we weren't getting along, their teamwork kind of slacked off, too.

Seth complained that he had to cook and collect food now that Summer and Jeremy were gone. Grant and Julia fought over who should carry more firewood. And Maleko was not happy about any of it.

The only person who has stayed neutral through all of this . . . is Dana!

"All right, people!" she said this morning after breakfast. "Just because this is the last day of Wild Hawaii doesn't mean we can all stop working. We still have to collect food for lunch, get more freshwater, and start packing up our stuff. Come on, team, move!"

Everyone grumbled and slowly got to their feet. Then we all started our chores.

"Thank you, Dana," Maleko said, smiling. "It's nice to see someone still remembers what teamwork is."

Who would have thought that Dana would be the one trying to pull the group together? I guess you just never know about people.

Dear Diary,

We're almost done! Even though we finished our work at the hotel a few days ago, Maleko put Elise, Summer, and me in charge of combing the campsite to make sure we didn't leave anything behind. So we're still hard at work.

"Hey, guys!" I told my friends as I pulled a stake out of the ground. "Think of it this way. If we hadn't done all this work outside we wouldn't be as totally buff and tan as we are right now. We look just like personal trainers."

Summer glanced at her tanned arms. A smile spread across her face. "I like the sound of that!" she said.

I had a special surprise for Elise. "Hey, Elise, you'll never believe what I learned," I said, picking a flower and holding it out to her. "If you rub this on your skin, your skin will automatically sparkle!"

"Really?" Elise said, taking the flower. She loves *anything* with glitter and sparkles.

Yay! I had managed to make both my friends happy!

That is, until Phoebe came over with her video camera. "I'm interviewing everyone for last-day thoughts," she explained, zooming in on us. "Elise, what do you have to say about Wild Hawaii?"

Elise's smile vanished. "I want to go home," she grumbled, dropping some tools into a box.

"I don't need to go home," Summer said into the camera. "I just really need a manicure!" She held out a hand with five broken fingernails.

"Maybe we need a break," I suggested. Then I eyed Phoebe's video camera. "Hey, Phoebe, did you interview Campbell yet?"

"No, why?" Phoebe asked.

"Can I do it for you?" I asked. "I'm a whiz with a video camera. And you can take a break, too."

Phoebe shrugged. "Okay." She handed me the camera.

Perfect, I thought. *Now I'll have an excuse to talk to Campbell about Mary-Kate.* I said good-bye to my friends and walked off in search of Campbell.

As I got closer to the trees, I heard a girl talking. "Maleko is sure to give me that hundred-dollar gift certificate for best teamwork now," she said. It was Dana!

I peeked from behind a tree. Dana was leaning against a palm branch talking on a cell phone.

"I can't believe I pulled it off, Kristen!" she said. "First I got Mary-Kate and Campbell to argue. Then I got everyone else fighting, too!"

I bet she's talking to Kristen Lindquist, I thought. Kristen was her best friend at White Oak.

I slinked around a few trees and rocks until I could see Dana, but I made sure she couldn't see me. I held up the video camera and pressed the Record button.

"I knew they were my worst competition for the gift certificate," Dana went on. "So I made them think that they were cursed by dumping their bait and oars into the lagoon. Then when Mary-Kate and I hiked to the volcano, I never asked Campbell to come along with us. But I told Mary-Kate that Campbell said she didn't want to go."

I was burning with anger. Mary-Kate was so wrong about Dana. Wild Hawaii hadn't changed her at all.

Dana giggled. "But the best was when I made sure Campbell never got this apology note Mary-Kate wrote her—and then I made it seem like Campbell stole Mary-Kate's fishing pole!"

Keep talking, I thought, as I zoomed the camera in on her. *Keep talking!*

Dana rocked back and forth with laughter. "I know. I was sure that if I acted really friendly with Mary-Kate, Campbell would get jealous. Am I good, or what?"

I'd heard enough. I clicked off the video camera and tiptoed away.

Chapter 13

Thursday

Dear Diary,

Around four o'clock, Maleko gathered the group one last time. He wanted to make his announcement about the winner for best teamwork. We all sat in a circle at the center of camp, waiting for him to speak.

"Okay," he said. "First of all, I hope you had fun at Wild Hawaii. You challenged yourselves every day and you should be proud of what you've accomplished here."

Everyone clapped.

Phoebe leaned over to me. "Ashley, can I have my video camera back?" she asked. "I should probably get this on tape."

"Just a sec," I whispered. "I need it for something really important."

"I'm sure you're dying to know," Maleko went on, "so let me cut to the chase and announce the winner of the Best Teamwork prize."

Everyone seemed pretty down in the dumps when Maleko said that. I could tell most of the group thought they hadn't been very good team players toward the end. But Dana was sitting up straight and smiling.

Maleko held up the gift certificate. "The winner for best teamwork is—Dana Woletsky!"

Dana stood up and flipped her dark brown hair over her shoulders. "Thank you so much!" she said, waving at everyone as if she were on a parade float or something. "I had such a great time with you all."

Oh, give me a break, I thought, and jumped to my feet.

"Wait a second," I said, holding out the video camera. "Can we watch this tape first?"

Dana stopped waving and glared at me. "Give it up, Ashley," she said. "You don't have to act jealous just because you got kicked out on the first day."

"What do you want to show us?" Maleko asked. He didn't seem to have much patience, so I rewound the tape and pressed Play.

Maleko and the other kids gathered around to watch the little screen on the video camera. The image of Dana talking on her cell phone appeared.

Dana gasped. "When did you tape that?"

I smiled at her and turned up the volume. Dana's recorded voice rang out. "Maleko is sure to give me that hundred-dollar gift certificate for best teamwork now. . . . But the best was when I made sure Campbell never got this apology note that Mary-Kate wrote her—and then I made it seem like Campbell stole Mary-Kate's fishing pole!"

"Stop!" Dana cried out. She turned to Maleko. "Ashley made that up! She faked it somehow. It's all because she hates me!"

Mary-Kate broke through the crowd and marched right up to Dana. "How *could* you!" she cried. "You pretended to be my friend, but you really just wanted to win the prize."

Campbell walked up behind Mary-Kate. Her cheeks were all red. "You're not going to get away with this," she said, pointing a finger in Dana's face. I pressed the Off button and handed the video camera to Maleko. It was game over for Dana Woletsky!

Dear Diary,

How could I have fallen for it? How could I not have realized that Dana is a big fat liar? She

actually made me believe that she was a better friend than Campbell was! And remember the garbage incident and the missing berries? Those were all thanks to Dana, too!

But on a happier note, now that the truth is out, I'm sure everything will be fine between Campbell and me again. As soon as I finish writing in you, Diary, I'm going to find her. I can't wait to make up!

Chapter 14

Friday

Dear Diary,

You will never guess what happened next. After all the excitement died down, a bunch of us decided to hang out by the pool at the hotel. Maleko came strolling over, holding the gift certificate in his hand.

"I've made my decision about the new winner for best teamwork," he announced.

Everyone stopped talking. Mary-Kate leaned over from the chair next to me. "I wonder who it's going to be," she whispered.

"Me, too," I whispered back. "Hey, maybe it's you!"

Mary-Kate shrugged. "I doubt it."

Maleko held up the gift certificate. "The winner is . . . Ashley Burke!" He looked straight at me.

I turned around. I figured there must have been another Ashley Burke sitting behind me, because there was no way Maleko was talking about me. I got kicked out of the game on day one!

"Yes, I mean you, Ashley,"

Maleko said, laughing at my reaction. "You deserve the prize."

"Why?" I asked, still confused.

Maleko handed the certificate to me. "Even though you made a mistake early on and had to leave the game, you more than made up for it by coming back to pitch in and bringing Summer and Elise with you."

"Wow, thanks!" I cried. Can you believe it, Diary?

Everyone came up to me and gave me high fives and big hugs. I went straight over to Summer and Elise.

"What do you say we all go on a Hawaiian shopping spree together?" I suggested. "We can split the prize three ways."

Elise's eyes lit up. "Thanks, Ashley."

Summer grinned. "Awesome!"

Isn't that excellent? Right after we left the pool, we went to the hotel boutiques. Summer chose a jar of pineapple facial cream, Elise bought a sparkly Hawaiian baby tee, and I got a new pair of cool-looking sunglasses. We all picked out a bunch of other souvenirs, too.

"I'm going to wear these for the next part of our Hawaiian vacation," I told Summer and Elise, slipping on my shades.

"We're going to a resort on another island. Kauai, right?" Summer said.

I nodded. "Right. And do you know what that means?"

Elise frowned. "What?"

I threw my arms into the air. "No more work!"

We all giggled like crazy as we left the store with a bunch of shopping bags.

My vacation in Hilo is going to have a happy ending after all! I thought.

Or maybe not. Leave it to Dana to burst my bubble. She approached me in the lobby right after Summer and Elise headed back to their room. "I need to talk to you," she said in a low voice.

"What do you want?" I asked. I was still angry at Dana for what she did to Mary-Kate.

Dana gave me a mean smile. "You ruined my trip. So now I'm going to ruin yours."

"What are you talking about?" I narrowed my eyes.

"I know a big secret about you," Dana said, smoothing down her pink skirt. "And when I tell everyone what it is, your vacation will be over."

I froze. "What secret?" I asked her, glancing around.

"You'll find out soon enough," Dana said. With that, she laughed and sauntered away.

What was she talking about? Did she really know something, or was she just lying again?

Dear Diary,

Diary, I have a HUGE problem!

Actually, *two* huge problems!

Now that Wild Hawaii is over and Ashley uncovered Dana's big plan, I thought that everything would be fine between Campbell and me.

But it's not.

Campbell didn't talk to me at all last night. She didn't talk to me this morning either. Every time I tried to speak to her, she made herself busy doing something else.

I didn't get it. "Campbell," I said as I watched her pack her suitcase. "I'm really really sorry about what happened. I should have never listened to Dana. Can't you accept my apology so we can be best friends again?"

Campbell slammed her suitcase shut and glared me. "No, I can't," she said coldly. "You accused me of stealing, and there's no excuse for that! There's also no excuse for believing all those awful things Dana said about me. Friends would never do that to each other—and *definitely* not best friends!"

She picked up her suitcase and headed for the door. "Sit with someone else on the boat, okay? And find someone else to share a room with in Kauai. Our friendship is history."

Diary, what am I going to do? I have to make Campbell forgive me!

Oh, and then there's my other problem.

Dana told Ashley that she knows a secret about her—one that's going to ruin her trip. Ashley doesn't know whether to believe her or not.

But I do. Dana is telling the truth. And the reason I know that is because . . . I'm the one who told her the secret!

What am I going to do?

Aloha!

PSST! Take a sneak peek
at

#24 Surf, Sand, and Secrets

Dear Diary,

Now that Wild Hawaii is over, there's only one thing to do. Relax! And the Hawaiian island of Kauai is the perfect place to do it!

I'm sitting in the lobby of the most amazing resort. It has free hula lessons, surfing lessons, water-skiing lessons—you name it! And we're going to do it all, just as soon as our chaperone, Ms. Clare, checks us in.

There's one thing ı m not happy about, though. My best friend, Campbell, is mad at me. I thought she stole something from me when she didn't. And even though I apologized, she still won't speak to me.

I looked up to see what Campbell was doing. But

before I could find her, I saw a tall man with short black hair walk by. Hey! He looked just like . . .

"Oh, wow!" I said. I jumped up and ran over to my sister, Ashley. She was leaning against the wall reading a magazine.

"Do you see who that is?" I asked.

She looked up and wrinkled her nose. "No, who is it?"

"It's Jake Nakamoto," I said. "He's one of the coolest, most famous baseball players in the world!"

"Oh," Ashley replied. She went back to reading her magazine.

Okay, so Ashley wasn't impressed by famous sports stars. But I was. And I knew someone else who was, too. Campbell!

I scanned the lobby until I found her. She was trying to see Jake over the people surrounding him.

Three big bodyguards waved the fans away from Jake. "Jake is not signing any autographs while he's at the resort!" one of the guards shouted.

Gee, that's harsh, I thought as I walked over to Campbell.

"Jake Nakamoto is my favorite baseball player," she was saying to Julia Langstrom, one of our classmates.

"Me, too," I added. "It's so cool that he's here!"

Campbell glanced at me, then turned back to

Julia. "Did you know that Jake's batting average was .350 last year? And he hit thirty home runs!"

Okay, okay, I got it. Campbell was ignoring me. But I wasn't going to give up.

"Remember when Jake hit that game-winning home run against Atlanta last season?" I asked.

No response. This time she didn't even look at me.

"Boy, I wish I could have his autograph," Campbell said to Julia. "It's such a bummer that he's not signing any."

That's it! I thought. *I'm going to get Jake Nakamoto's autograph for Campbell. Then she'll have to forgive me!*

I glanced at the mean-looking bodyguards surrounding Jake. The only question was . . . how?

Dear Diary,

My friend, Phoebe, has been acting really weird lately. So tonight, after dinner, I decided to go talk to her and see what was going on. I found her in one of the elaborate hotel gardens, looking through a big telescope.

"Hey, Phoebe," I said.

Phoebe straightened up so fast that she almost bonked her head on the telescope. "Oh, um . . . hi."

"What are you looking at?" I asked, gesturing to the telescope.

"I'm looking at . . . the stars," Phoebe replied.

I glanced up at the sky. "Phoebe, the stars aren't out," I said. "It's not dark yet."

Phoebe shifted nervously. Obviously she didn't want to talk about what she was doing. I decided to change the topic for now.

"So there's a poetry reading on the beach tonight," I said. "Do you want to go?"

Phoebe loved poetry. She even decorated our dorm room with posters of famous poets!

But Phoebe shook her head. "No, thanks. I don't feel like listening to poetry tonight." She bent down and looked through the telescope again.

Huh? Phoebe was turning down a night of poetry? Now I knew something was wrong.

"Phoebe, are you sure nothing is bothering you?" I asked. "You've been acting really—"

Phoebe gasped. "No way!" she cried, backing away from the telescope. Then she took off running.

"Phoebe, wait!" I called. But she didn't stop.

What had she seen in the telescope? I wondered. I looked through the lens. But all I saw were a bunch of waiters walking out of the hotel kitchen.

Now I was totally confused. What had made Phoebe freak out like that?

Win a Mary-Kate and Ashley Fun in the Sun Gift Pack!

ENTER BELOW TO WIN EVERYTHING YOU NEED FOR A GREAT DAY AT THE BEACH!

- A portable stereo system
- Mary-Kate and Ashley Greatest Hits and Greatest Hits II music CDs
- An autographed Mary-Kate and Ashley summer reading library
- Mary-Kate and Ashley brand sunglasses, beach towel, beach ball and T-shirt
- Much, much more…

Mail to: **MARY-KATE AND ASHLEY FUN IN THE SUN GIFT PACK SWEEPSTAKES**
C/O HarperEntertainment
Attention: Children's Marketing Department
10 East 53rd Street, New York, NY 10022

No purchase necessary.

Name: _____

Address: _____

City: _____ State: _____ Zip: _____

Phone: _____ Age: _____

HarperEntertainment
An Imprint of HarperCollinsPublishers
www.harpercollins.com

The Books for Real Girls

America Online
mary-kateandashley.com
America Online Keyword: mary-kateandashley

PARACHUTE PRESS

DUALSTAR PUBLICATIONS

TWO OF A KIND™
Mary-Kate & Ashley Fun in the Sun Gift Pack Sweepstakes

OFFICIAL RULES:

1. No purchase necessary.

2. To enter complete the official entry form or hand print your name, address, age, and phone number along with the words "TWO OF A KIND Fun in the Sun Sweepstakes" on a 3" x 5" card and mail to: TWO OF A KIND Fun in the Sun Sweepstakes, c/o HarperEntertainment, Attn: Children's Marketing Department, 10 East 53rd Street, New York, NY 10022. Entries must be received **no later than October 31, 2002.** Enter as often as you wish, but each entry must be mailed separately. One entry per envelope. Partially completed, illegible, or mechanically reproduced entries will not be accepted. Sponsors are not responsible for lost, late, mutilated, illegible, stolen, postage due, incomplete, or misdirected entries. All entries become the property of Dualstar Entertainment Group, Inc., and will not be returned.

3. Sweepstakes open to all legal residents of the United States (excluding Colorado & Rhode Island) who are between the ages of five and fifteen on October 31, 2002, excluding employees and immediate family members of HarperCollins Publishers, Inc., ("HarperCollins"), Warner Bros.Television ("Warner"), Parachute Properties and Parachute Press, Inc., and their respective subsidiaries and affiliates, officers, directors, shareholders, employees, agents, attorneys, and other representatives (individually and collectively "Parachute"), Dualstar Entertainment Group, Inc., and its subsidiaries and affiliates, officers, directors, shareholders, employees, agents, attorneys, and other representatives (individually and collectively "Dualstar"), and their respective parent companies, affiliates, subsidiaries, advertising, promotion and fulfillment agencies, and the persons with whom each of the above are domiciled. Offer void where prohibited or restricted by law.

4. Odds of winning depend on the total number of entries received. Approximately 525,000 sweepstakes notifications published. Prize will be awarded. Winner will be randomly drawn on or about November 15, 2002, by HarperEntertainment, whose decisions are final. Potential winner will be notified by mail and will be required to sign and return an affidavit of eligibility and release of liability within 14 days of notification. Prize won by minors will be awarded to parent or legal guardian who must sign and return all required legal documents. By acceptance of the prize, winners consent to the use of their names, photographs, likeness, and personal information by HarperCollins, Parachute, Dualstar, and for publicity purposes without further compensation except where prohibited.

5. One (1) Grand Prize Winner wins a Mary-Kate and Ashley Fun in the Sun Gift Pack, consisting of the following: a portable stereo, MARY-KATE AND ASHLEY GREATEST HITS and GREATEST HITS II music CDs, Mary-Kate and Ashley beach towel, Mary-Kate and Ashley beach ball, Mary-Kate and Ashley T-Shirt, Mary-Kate and Ashley brand sunglasses, an autographed Mary-Kate and Ashley summer reading library of five books, beach hat, beach bag, glitter lip gloss. Approximate retail value: $450.00

6. Only one prize will be awarded per individual, family, or household. Prize is non-transferable and cannot be sold or redeemed for cash. No cash substitute is available. Any federal, state, or local taxes are the responsibility of the winner. Sponsor may substitute prize of equal or greater value, if necessary, due to availability.

7. Additional terms: By participating, entrants agree a) to the official rules and decisions of the judges, which will be final in all respects; and to waive any claim to ambiguity of the official rules and b) to release, discharge, and hold harmless HarperCollins, Warner, Parachute, Dualstar, and their affiliates, subsidiaries, and advertising and promotion agencies from and against any and all liability or damages associated with acceptance, use, or misuse of any prize received in this sweepstakes.

8. Any dispute arising from this Sweepstakes will be determined according to the laws of the State of New York, without reference to its conflict of law principles, and the entrants consent to the personal jurisdiction of the State and Federal courts located in New York County and agree that such courts have exclusive jurisdiction over all such disputes.

9. To obtain the name of the winner, please send your request and a self-addressed stamped envelope (excluding residents of Vermont and Washington) to TWO OF A KIND Fun in the Sun Sweepstakes, c/o HarperEntertainment, Attn: Children's Marketing Department, 10 East 53rd Street, New York, NY 10022 by December 1, 2002. Sweepstakes Sponsor: HarperCollins Publishers, Inc.

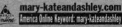

Reading Checklist

andashley

single one!

- ❏ It's a Twin Thing
- ❏ How to Flunk
  Your First Date
- ❏ The Sleepover Secret
- ❏ One Twin Too Many
- ❏ To Snoop or Not to Snoop?
- ❏ My Sister the Supermodel
- ❏ Two's a Crowd
- ❏ Let's Party!
- ❏ Calling All Boys
- ❏ Winner Take All
- ❏ P. S. Wish You Were Here
- ❏ The Cool Club
- ❏ War of the Wardrobes
- ❏ Bye-Bye Boyfriend
- ❏ It's Snow Problem
- ❏ Likes Me, Likes Me Not
- ❏ Shore Thing
- ❏ Two for the Road

- ❏ Surprise, Surprise
- ❏ Sealed With a Kiss
- ❏ Now You See Him, Now you Don't
- ❏ April Fools' Rules!

so little time

- ❏ How to Train a Boy
- ❏ Instant Boyfriend
- ❏ Too Good To Be True

- ❏ Never Been Kissed
- ❏ Wishes and Dreams
- ❏ The Perfect Summer

Super Specials:
- ❏ My Mary-Kate & Ashley Diary
- ❏ Our Story
- ❏ Passport to Paris Scrapbook
- ❏ Be My Valentine

**Available wherever books are sold,
or call 1-800-331-3761 to order.**

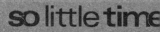

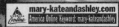

 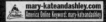